Mallory got up and headed for the door

The sun was tingeing the sky, awakening shadows that had lain dormant under the moon. As she reached the living room, Brad called her name. She turned back as he stretched himself out of the chair and came toward her. Mallory watched him move. His gait was sure, predatory, catlike, quiet. She held her breath. She'd never been this affected by a man before.

"Thank you," he said.

"Get some sleep," she said, breaking the tension, knowing that there was no way she would be getting much herself. Not with thoughts of Dr. Brad Clayton filling her head...and her heart.

Shirley Hailstock
LOVE ON CALL

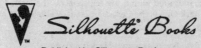
Silhouette Books

Published by Silhouette Books
America's Publisher of Contemporary Romance

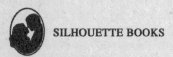 **SILHOUETTE BOOKS**

ISBN 0-373-28550-7

LOVE ON CALL

Copyright © 2004 by Shirley Hailstock

Books by Shirley Hailstock

Silhouette Special Edition

A Father's Fortune #1521
Love on Call #1594

SHIRLEY HAILSTOCK

is the author of over fourteen books and novellas. She has received numerous awards for her work, including the Holt Medallion, the Barclay Gold Award and the Golden Quill Award. *Romantic Times BOOK club* awarded her a Career Achievement Award and one of her books made the Top 100 Romances of the 20th Century List.

Shirley loves to sew and bake, but she can't find the time to sew and baking is way too fattening. She loves to hear from fans. You can write her at P.O. Box 513, Plainsboro, NJ 08536 or browse her Web site at http://www.geocities.com/shailstock.

To my sister Wygenia Miles, my greatest publicist.
She carries a cheat sheet of my titles in her purse
and never misses an opportunity to push my books.
All my thanks.

Chapter One

Dr. Mallory Russell should have been home with her feet up and a cold glass of cranberry-orange juice at her side. Her shift had ended three hours ago, but tonight was one for the record books. The emergency room looked like they were giving away money. There were more patients than she'd ever seen without a major accident or some natural disaster, and the place was jam-packed. It was nearly midnight now, and she'd been on her feet for fourteen hours.

After picking up the chart of the next patient, she rolled her neck to ease the tension in her shoulders. She couldn't stifle the yawn that reminded her she craved sleep. Then she stared at the vitals on the chart.

"What do we have here?" she asked one of the

two police officers standing next to the curtain of bed five. Officers Percy and Winkler showed up in Emergency at least once a week. The night wouldn't be the same without seeing them. She continued to scan the chart that accompanied the newest patient.

"Junkie," Officer Winkler said. "Flying on something." His voice held neither censure or judgment.

"Knife wound on the neck," Percy added. "We found him lying on the ground about a mile from here. He was so out of it he couldn't even speak."

"He's unconscious so we took the restraints off," Officer Winkler said, following Mallory into the sectioned-off bay.

She nodded at them. Jane Ellerby looked up as Mallory entered. The RN was cleaning the patient's wound. She picked up the stainless steel bowl with blood-stained water and discarded swabs and left them alone.

"What's his name?" Mallory asked. She hadn't looked at the name when she'd checked the medical treatment that had already been administered to him.

"Wayne Mason," Officer Percy answered.

"Is he a regular?" He'd said the name so matter-of-factly that Mallory thought he knew it.

"He's got a rap sheet as long as your arm. Mostly petty stuff. Last couple of years he's been into drugs."

"All right, wait outside."

Mallory swung the curtain around the track as they left her alone with the unconscious man. She looked at his neck first. The cut wasn't deep enough to sever anything vital but it came close. Another millimeter and he would be in surgery.

She checked his face, carefully observing everything she could about him. He had many scars visible. Some of them were pretty old, probably from childhood. He looked to be in his twenties. So young, she thought.

Pulling his eyelids up, she checked his pupils. They were pinpoints, and his eyes were glassy. He was coming down. He'd spent a lot of money for his fifteen-minute high and the chance to permanently kill off brain cells, and he wasn't even awake to feel it.

She checked his pulse and blood pressure. His heart was beating like a hummingbird, much too fast. His blood pressure was high enough for him to go into convulsions.

Suddenly his eyes flew open. Wildly, he stared around the room, his head whipping from side to side. He started to get up. Mallory put her hands on his shoulders to prevent him from rising.

"You're all right," she whispered in a calming voice she'd mastered over the years. "You're in the hospital. I'm your doctor." Mallory had no idea if he understood her in his state. He continued to look anxiously around the room. "You're all right," she said again.

His eyes were still wild, afraid, shifting rapidly. Mallory had dealt with junkies before. In this hospital they were common. The nurses even referred to it as the "police hospital." Stabbings, gunshot wounds, burns from house fires and emergencies involving the police were usually directed to Philadelphia General.

Wayne Mason grunted. While the sound was low, it had the underlying tone of a wounded animal. Mallory raised her hand to reassure him. He grabbed her wrist, wrenching it so tightly she cried out. He swung his legs over the side of the gurney and sat up, still holding on to her. She struggled and he pulled her back. A metal pan crashed to the floor. The man slid off the gurney, swinging her around and tugging her against him in almost the same movement. He was incredibly strong, and he was holding her in a painful position that rendered her helpless. If she could only get him off balance, she could get away.

She opened her mouth to scream, but the thought was cut off when she felt the knife against her throat.... '

The sound of a metal pan dropping somewhere on the other side of the curtain didn't jar Dr. Bradley Clayton's hand by a centimeter. He was used to emergency room medicine. He wasn't scheduled for duty, but had come in to help out when he'd heard the workload was high.

"Can I have it back now?" He smiled at the child playing with his small flashlight. The child shone the light in his eyes and Brad lifted up his hands as if aliens were throwing the death ray in his direction. The rosy-cheeked boy laughed, obviously playful despite the late hour.

"You can go home now." Brad glanced at the

child's mother. "I've written a prescription for him. You can fill it tomorrow. He'll be fine for the rest of the night."

The mother looked relieved. She placed her arm around her son's shoulders and looked down at him.

Suddenly another tray dropped. Beyond the curtain feet shuffled and then someone screamed.

"Stay with him," Brad ordered the mother. Instinctively he knew something had gotten out of hand. He pulled the curtain aside and stepped into the fray.

Pandemonium greeted him. People were everywhere: patients, nurses, orderlies. Even two uniformed policemen, both pulling their guns out of holsters. The whole room seemed to be hopping. Carts rolled freely as their stunned custodians forgot to keep hold of them. Then Brad saw *her*.

"Stop!" the man holding the knife yelled. "I'll kill her," he said, directing his speech to the two officers.

Brad stepped forward. The man shifted toward him, whipping Dr. Russell around as if she were a doll. Her eyes met Brad's. "Don't anybody move," the man said. The room fell silent, everyone stopped where they were.

Brad glanced again at the officers, then back at the young doctor. Mallory had her free hand out to the crowd, appearing to hold them back instead of clutching the man's arm in an attempt to keep him from slitting her throat. Brad would never have expected that.

"Put the knife down, Wayne," one of the officers said.

"No one needs to get hurt here," the other stated.

"Man, I ain't stupid," the junkie snarled. "You're just dying to hurt me," he told them. "Now, put down the guns."

"Wayne," Mallory said softly. Brad kept his eyes on her. A stream of blood ran in a line from under her left ear down her throat, to soak into the white blouse she wore under her medical coat. "Wayne, it's going to be all right. Isn't it, Wayne?"

"If nobody moves. I don't want to kill anybody," Wayne answered. "But I will," he insisted in a loud voice.

"Wayne, you were hurt. I need to check your injuries."

"No," he said. Sweat was pouring off him. Brad didn't know if that was good or bad. It would bring him down faster, but it could freak him out, make him lose control of his reflexes.

"What could it hurt?" Mallory asked.

"It's a trick," Wayne said.

Brad wasn't sure. Did she have something up her sleeve?

"You were brought here because you need help. This is a hospital," she murmured.

Mallory Russell was trying to reason with an addict. Brad knew she couldn't. He took an involuntary step toward them.

"You've been warned once." The man faced Brad. His voice was cold, confident and deadly. Mallory's eyes seemed to plead with Brad to do nothing. Wayne glanced back at the cops. "You," he said. "Put them on the floor."

They knew better than to try to shoot in a room full of people. Both uniformed policemen bent down and placed their guns in front of them.

"Stand up," the man ordered. They stood. "Kick them over here." As they moved to follow the order, he added, "One at a time. And slowly." They did as he asked. Wayne stopped each one with his foot.

"Wayne." Mallory spoke again. "How are you feeling?"

"What do you care?"

"I'm your doctor. I care." He grunted at her. "The police brought you in because your heart was beating too fast."

Brad watched her. She had guts.

"Your heart, Wayne." she paused. "You don't want to die, do you?"

He hesitated. The word seemed to penetrate his drug-crazed mind.

Brad wanted to move, wanted to do something, but he didn't know what. The room was too crowded. And he'd been warned. Equipment and people stood between him and the knife-wielding man.

"If you let me take your pulse I can see if the medicine is working," she said.

"Medicine? What medicine?"

"While you were out, I gave you an injection. Can't you feel where the needle pricked your arm?"

"What did you give me?"

"Nothing that would hurt you," she rushed to explain. "It was to help steady your heart. But I need to check—"

"No," he shouted, cutting her off.

"Wayne, you have the knife. And my arm, which hurts, by the way."

Brad could see him relax his grip, although he didn't let go completely. Mallory seemed to relax a little, too.

"Thanks," she said. Some of the color returned to her face and she appeared to have confidence in what she was planning. He still didn't know what that was, but it was surely dangerous. "Now I need to take your pulse."

The addict said nothing.

"Wayne, I need to turn around."

"This isn't a trick?"

"This isn't a trick."

He looked around the E.R., checking where everyone was. His eyes lit on Brad with a coldness that could crack teeth. Then he stared at the cops. "Move and she's history," he said. Both men raised their hands, palms up, showing they understood.

The man watched the room for what seemed like an eon. Then he quickly moved the knife, turned Mallory around, twisted her arm behind her and placed the knife under her right ear.

"Go ahead," he said.

"I can't do it with this hand."

"Then it won't be done." Her body was tightly wedged against his. Her head only reached his chin. Brad felt a strong urge to grab her and pull her free.

Mallory sighed, and Brad wished he knew what she was up to.

"Can I raise my free hand? I'll take your pulse under your chin."

Then Brad knew. There was only one thing she could try from where she was standing. He was stunned. She can't do it, he thought. It was crazy to even attempt it. Yet it was the only option he could see.

With her left hand Mallory placed her fingers on the man's carotid artery and pressed. In seconds the addict's eyes rolled into his head. The knife slipped from his hand and clattered to the floor. The fingers holding Mallory's right arm behind her back went slack. The man passed out.

She'd done it.

Mallory took his weight as he fell on her. She stepped back, trying to brace herself, struggled to keep him upright, but his limp body was too much for her and they both collapsed to the floor. That seemed to be the catalyst for everyone else in the room to sigh in relief, then leap into action. The two cops moved first, rushing toward Mallory, scooping their guns up as they went. Carts crashed and people rushed forward. Someone screamed. Someone else gasped.

Brad himself hastened forward as the cops pulled the junkie off of her.

"Wait," she shouted over the din that filled the room. Getting to her knees, she bent over the man she'd just rendered helpless, and checked his heart-beat and his breathing.

Brad knew there was nothing she could prescribe without knowing what was already in his blood chemistry. He was sure the man hadn't been in the hospital long enough for her to have given him an injection. So she was checking to see that cutting off the blood to his brain had not killed him.

"He's alive," she sighed in relief. "Get him back on the gurney."

Mallory stood up. Everyone was looking at her. She suddenly appeared uncomfortable, more now than she had when she was being threatened with death.

"It's all over now," she announced, and headed for the room where they were taking the addict.

Brad caught her then, curling his fingers around her arm. He expected to find soft tissue, but his hand closed over strong, firm muscles, well-toned. Mallory pulled her arm away.

"You can't go in there," he said.

"He's *my* patient."

Brad glanced behind her and saw Dr. Mark Peterson.

"Would you take over?" he asked without her permission. Mark nodded and headed toward the addict.

"You have no right," she said.

"True," he agreed. "But you could be in shock."

She was good in an emergency, she'd just proved that. And she could think on her feet. Now that the drama had ended he expected the natural reaction: